SOS

MISSING

Tales From The UK

Edited By Donna Samworth

First published in Great Britain in 2020 by:

 Young**Writers**® — Est. 1991 —

Young Writers
Remus House
Coltsfoot Drive
Peterborough
PE2 9BF
Telephone: 01733 890066
Website: www.youngwriters.co.uk

Printed and bound in the UK by BookPrintingUK
Website: www.bookprintinguk.com
YB0446JX

FOREWORD

IF YOU'VE BEEN SEARCHING FOR EPIC ADVENTURES, TALES OF SUSPENSE AND IMAGINATIVE WRITING THEN SEARCH NO MORE! YOU'VE FOUND WHAT YOU'VE BEEN LOOKING FOR WITH THIS ANTHOLOGY OF MINI SAGAS.

We challenged secondary school students to craft a story in just 100 words. In this second installment of our SOS Sagas, their mission was to write on the theme of 'Missing'. They were encouraged to think beyond their first instincts and explore deeper into the theme. The result is a variety of styles and genres and, as well as some classic lost and found tales, inside these pages you may find characters looking for meaning, memories erased or even whole populations disappearing overnight.

Here at Young Writers it's our aim to inspire the next generation and instill in them a love of creative writing, and what better way than to see their work in print? The imagination and skill within these pages are proof that we might just be achieving that aim! Well done to each of these fantastic authors.

CONTENTS

Katie Bailey (12)	70	Junior De Carvalho Rosa (12)	112
Aseda Adusei	71	Mofijinfoluwa Olayiwola (11)	113
Valentina Innamorati (13)	72	Polychronia Maria Moschouris (15)	114
Syaam Hussain (12)	73		
Cole Carrick (13)	74	Logan Wilson (14)	115
Ramani Mattu (13)	75	Coby Drew (13)	116
Maddison Arscott (12)	76	Harry Martin (12)	117
Geovana Maziero Camarotto (13)	77	Macie Real	118
		Isla Ennis-Smillie	119
Kamil Szakiel (15)	78	Cai Williams (11)	120
Hannah Lynch	79	Jesper Fitzsimmons	121
Fatima Iftikhar (13)	80	Aziza Khan	122
Molly Godfrey (13)	81	Azaria Scott (15)	123
Shana-Leigh Fellows (15)	82	Evelyn Kenrick (15)	124
Sushant Shyam (13)	83	Zainab Soogun	125
Arnav Kasireddy (12)	84	Rytham Rasalawala (12)	126
Raissa Hirji (13)	85	Inayah Abbasi	127
Sanyia Choudhury (12)	86	Gene Simmonds (16)	128
Deanna Jebouri (12)	87	Lilian Turner (16)	129
Katie Bartlett	88	Arzoo Nori (14)	130
Evie McIntosh (13)	89	Alex Delahaye (12)	131
Gergana Manolova (15)	90	Noah Robinson (16)	132
Evan Palmer (12)	91	Alexia Wilson (13)	133
Serena Cooper (14)	92	Anya-Grace Nembhard (14)	134
Jordan Giannasi	93	Mia Rock (13)	135
Anya Trofimova	94	Joanna Odumusi (14)	136
Evie Hodgson (14)	95	Tyler Dewick-Wilson	137
Arnesh Srivastava (12)	96	Lewis Nzekwe (12)	138
Max Pattison (12)	97	Hollie Mae Hughes (13)	139
Alexander Rate (13)	98	Erin Taylor (11)	140
Thaya Warren (16)	99	Riya Swaminathan (12)	141
Fenet Chemir (13)	100	Basar Kizildere (12)	142
Baveena Selvanendam (13)	101	Thalia Shola Remice (14)	143
Powlo Remice (12)	102	Oliver Kent (13)	144
Libby Rix (13)	103	Summer Mead	145
Delina Vithani (12)	104	Oliver Lovelock (12)	146
Tricia Currie (15)	105	Serena Whittlestone (15)	147
Ganesh Mistry (15)	106	Sophie Gillin (13)	148
Armaan Raheel	107	Sophie Edwards (12)	149
Rola Al-Hassani (11)	108	Siân Phillips	150
Sophie Ryder (12)	109	Isabelle Embleton	151
Archie Lewis (11)	110	Reece Walker (12)	152
Hannah Jayne Bennett (14)	111	Hiba Kola (13)	153

Mahdiya Noor Mahmood (13)	154
Amelie Coote (11)	155
Meghan Coleborn (15)	156
Oliver Burrow (12)	157
Sophia Nelson (13)	158
Mya Kent (12)	159
Amelia Drummond-Harris (11)	160
Joana Cabaca	161
Finn Shuttleworth (10)	162
Morgan Mates (11)	163
Abdullah Ahmad (12)	164
Mateea Sivriu (19)	165
Amelia Lewis (12)	166
Aarna Patel (12)	167
Caitlyn Gallagher-Blake (11)	168
Jimisola Okuwobi (12)	169
Leon Gamper (11)	170
Monty Hulbert (12)	171
Rubi Merrell (13)	172
Khrish Deugi (12)	173
Naideen Elle Dailly (12)	174
Brandon Ellis	175
Dane Brett (12)	176
Jessica Williamson (13)	177
Cohyn Williams (12)	178
Eryk Grzegorz Wojewodzki (13)	179
Fikile Soko (11)	180
Evie May Phipps (13)	181
Hawwaa' Bint Mahmood (16)	182

THE STORIES

SCP-3000

Officer Falbrough has been missing for five days after entering subject SCP-3000 containment facility. She entered the facility believing there to be a disturbance. The following is a transcript of the radio conversation.

Basecamp: "Falbrough, do you copy?"

Falbrough: "Falbrough here sir, I see the subj... Oh god..."

Basecamp: "What's going on officer?"

Falbrough: "God... there appears to be an eel, several kilometres long, where SCP-2500 should be... It's staring at me... No... Please no!"

Basecamp: "Officer, you are with SCP-3000. Evacuate the facility immediately. I repeat, evacuate immediately!"

(Repeated screaming was heard before Homebase lost contact with Falbrough.)

Jessica Morgan Whitford (14)

Found You

They've found me. Me, the missing human. The escaped human.

The last human.

I run, run through the white corridors, gulping for air, trying to breathe. They're catching up. Their engines thundering, blaring, their alarms screaming into my ears, flashing a bright, crimson blood-red.

I'm drowning.

Suffocating.

Asphyxiating.

I stumble into a lab, my breathing ragged, my vision distorted. Outside the noise slowly dies down. The room becomes quiet, deathly quiet.

The silence is unnerving.

And then that's when I hear it. Behind me. The dull beeping, the lifeless, artificial voice, and then, in that tell-tale, childish tone: 'Found you'.

Lindsey Zhou (13)

A Shattered Heirloom

Heavily, the thunderous rain poured from the depressing, stormy clouds. Meanwhile, I frantically searched my house after an outlandish disappearance from the impenetrable safe. Unfortunately, my ancestor's cherished, priceless heirloom was nowhere to be found. A miserable tear gradually drifted down my cheek and I could hear nothing but the rapid throb of my shattered heart. I gulped. Apprehensively, I decided to take another inspection, looking out for three topaz diamonds pierced into the glamorous, golden, gifted heirloom. After a while, my eyes widened at the scandalizing sight of three familiar but pulverized topaz gems. I staggeringly whispered, "Oh no."

Japji Kaur Grewal (12)

Missing

'Body found 300 yards away from home!'
'Human remains found, decomposing!'
'Concern grows for missing boy!'
All those recent cases. All those lives lost. All near David
Brooke's house. In fact, they seem to be getting nearer...
"David, I hope you're doing your homework..."
Frantically, David scrambles to hide the evidence he was
about to put on his corkboard. Images of smiling people
that were pronounced dead or missing that very morning.
His mother looked at him sorrowfully. "Obsessing over the
fact that they're dead won't bring them back."
With a sigh, David shakes his head. "Might as well try."

Emilia Gloria Iskra (13)

The Invisible Cry

'Missing?' The poster's corners flapped indignantly in the wind. A reflection.

'Missing: Mary Matthews'.

Icily, sinful rays of sunshine danced with the malevolent wind. Clustered cars roared like savage animals while trees beheld their humanity arrogantly. Silence.

It suddenly happened so fast. Cars barred their bright teeth towards me. My petrified body couldn't move. Closer... closer... closer, they came! Echoes of laden shrieks from my mouth bounced sinisterly into my eardrums only. Hell was Earth, Earth was Hell. They engulfed me mercilessly. Then, they passed. That's when I realised: no one could see me. I was the girl.

Filothea Petric (16)

A Million To One

His gaunt fingers wiped away the bittersweet taste of blood as the cold mist of the winter's howl struck his shivering body. Oblivious to his surroundings, he stood up, his eyes fluttering open to the unusual surrounding. The harsh stench of damp, overgrown foliage plummeted on to him, his gaze pondering over the surroundings. *Impossible*, the word repeating in his head. Where once were worn pavements beaten by polished shoes, were cracks and pioneering weeds. Where once were skyscrapers smudged by pollution, were standing tombstones colonised by lichen and ivy. Where once were millions of beating hearts, now remained one...

Josh Ethan Obi

Army Invasion

At the Alaska Army Base 0700, soldiers were picking up a surprising interference in their network (it was suspected it was an invasion). Commander Dage shouted, "Soldiers get ready! Go! Go! Go!"

It was too late, the invasion started. Abruptly, the soldiers rushed out to protect the base. Unfortunately, the other force too powerful, they obliterate the army base into smithereens.

Several minutes later, after the attack, Commander Dage weakly wakes up with a couple, other comrades. Abruptly, they start drifting up to the aircraft.

When the search crew arrives there is no sight of them. Where have they gone?

Gokula Krishna Madhukar (12)

Sailing Comes With A Price

Without a sound, the overpowering ocean snatched the toy boat. Rearing the satanic storm wiped out Earth. The impenetrable abyss of darkness was a black whole: inescapable! The disfigured ship drew towards hell, to be spat out again for the ocean's entertainment. The crew: lathered in sweat; rushing with adrenaline, their stench was as nauseating as the corpse flower.
Rising slowly the Kraken awakened. Now it was the Devil's playground ensuing work for idle hands. Usurping the momentaneous area the sea covered, the menacing creature killed everything in its path: not a soul spared... Blood spiced the air!

Shri Ritesh Pankhania (12)

The Accident At Wonderworld

Wonderworld, a place where you can fly magic carpets, become a wizard and speak to animals. Wonderworld is the happiest place on Earth. *Was!* All the joy ended after that day...

People got on, ready to experience the fastest theme park ride in England. They raced into a tunnel, but didn't come out. Emergency services could not answer the frantic questions asked. No screams. No holes. No smoke. Nothing. The world began making theories; they had no evidence. Nobody was blamed because everyone was clueless. Police interrogated all suspects; they knew nothing. So answer me this reader... Where are they?

Annie Shackleton (14)

Alien

She observed it closely, its moss-green face was softly crumpled and it had a tiny creased seaweed-green mouth and large mysterious eyes glittering like black pools of space, almost as if you could go in and find galaxies of lost things and twinkling stars. A ripple through of tranquil unknown buzzed through her, an indescribable feeling which roughly translated to "Do you want to know a secret?" She nodded then a curtain of silvery hair swished between them, her warm breath whispered into its shrivelled ear. Another tranquil vibration through her. "I'm where all the lost things go..."

Annabel Bradley (13)

Inexplicable

The city was derelict: a ghost town, abandoned, creepy. Whatever you may utter. All was gone. Everyone. The skyscrapers still stood there looming
above; they knew that the bustling bodies that usually squirmed within them had evacuated. I remember my monotonous mooch around the
place, purely just to escape my apartment, the hive of activity that I had just taken for granted, the noise I had taken for granted had disappeared as quick as anything. "Hellooooo!" it echoed.
My body sank lower and lower onto the concrete. Salty, emotional tears streamed down my face, stinging my gashes of war. Help!

Rosie Mantle

Voices In His Head

It all began with the humming the night after Uncle Ben died, the vibrations engulfing his ears and retreating to his skull, aggressively pounding against temples, summoning him to close his miserable eyes and succumb to the voices. But if he did, there was no going back, so he kept them open, wide with fear and glistening with disbelief.
"Robert, close your eyes," they hissed enticingly, "join your Uncle Ben."
The voices echoed so piercingly that Robert was certain the whole house could hear them. And suddenly, they stopped. Convinced, Robert closed his eyes, only to never wake up again.

Gunjan Randhawa (17)

The Hunt

They'll never find me. The musty room, clouded with dust. Cobwebs lurking. Stomach-churning memories stalking my past. I couldn't own up to my crime. I sat there, still as the person I'd killed. Suddenly, *creak*. Panicking, I stumbled towards the cracked window. My shaky breath choked me as a figure appeared, relishing my fear. Eyes widening, I scrabbled at the latch. The window swung open and robust wind whistled ferociously. Chills crawled up my spine as I gawped at the never-ending drop. No time, I had to jump. Tumbling. Screaming. Until... blackout. The end of my nightmares and guilt.

Amelie Carter (11)

John Claude

This was the third unsuccessful case of the week for John Claude. However, he knew that the missing bodies were all connected because he had a very dire and sinister secret. The main hunch was the victims seemed to disappear two days after each other. John Claude concluded that the killer was highly sophisticated as they left no traces. Arnold, John's assistant, arrived on scene and stated, "You know another death might be today? Last one was two days ago." John replied, "I know." A smile crept up onto his face. Arnold, confused, said, "What's funny? Argh!"

John Samuel (13)

Purgatory

"Hello?" No response.

"Hello!" Still no response.

She was, at first, falling down, down down, for what seemed like forever. Then, she woke up in this mysterious place. It was white and seemed to stretch out forever.

She had no idea where she was, but something told her that she wouldn't be getting an answer anytime soon.

"Well, hello, there." She turned to the sudden sound of a deep, gravelly voice.

Walking towards her was a figure shrouded in a black cloak. The hood of the cloak covered their face, so she didn't know who it was.

"You're here early..."

Jo-Andrea Mirembe (18)

The Girl Who Disappeared

February 2000, a girl named Abigail took her bookbag and walked out of her house. At 6:30am her mother discovered she was 'missing'. Police believe she left the house on her own, but Abigail's disappearance wasn't 'normal'. Several people spotted Abigail crying down the highway in the early hours of the morning. A few went to see if she was okay, but Abigail evaporated into black smoke almost like a ghost. Searches found nothing.

One year later, her bookbag was discovered but Abigail was never seen again. The funny thing is... Hi, I'm Abigail and this is my story.

Ellie Laggan (12)

Strayed In The Pure Emptiness

Interrupted by the blizzard there was no way to know which direction was right; the usual landmarks were obscured behind the linen whiteness that swirled so densely. Part of me was missing as no sounds were echoed into the surroundings and not even a solemn breeze in the lonesome air. *Crackle.* The ice shifted apprehensively as it disintegrated and weakened in the morning sun, melting as the warmth slowly parted the chunky ice. Perniciously the ice drifted further away from land into the middle of nowhere like incense. They'll never find me... the view was empty. Fear somnambulated around.

Claudia Anton (16)

Faded Away

I'd lost something. I wasn't sure what, but... lights flooded into my half-opened eyes as I blinked away empty nightmares and meaningless dreams. I looked around the room and realised I had no idea where I was.
A lady in uniform walked in. "I'm glad to see you're awake, they were very worried."
My mind was blank, as if shrouded by a dark veil. I couldn't think straight.
Who was she talking about?
Two strangers entered the room, tears cascading down their cheeks. "Oh Lizzy, we've missed you."
I stared in disbelief. The lost thing. No! Was it my memory?

Gabriella Smith (13)

On The Investigation Of The Disappearance Of Franklin Patrick Clark, 1922

By the hour of twenty-three, the investigation had been called off. Like the final piece of a puzzle when nearing completion, FP Clark had vanished. Who did remain - in part - his wife, whom had been suspended from the chandelier in his most extravagant ballroom as a most disturbing, deceased ornament, afflicting a most terrible stain of red upon the rug. *Foul*, the detective thought, noting but one of his colleagues had returned. No reply came of his shouted query, though the opened window, bloodied blade and missing colleague suggested that FP Clark was not quite as missing as hoped.

Sam Webb (17)

Captured

Now 3am. The four boys are set up to do a seance. Camera rolling. They join hands and Colby starts the seance. They sit in silence for a moment then hear a massive bang. They investigate. Then Colby screams and goes missing. The ransom note arrives and says where they can find Colby. The note was from Satan.

"I can't believe I'd missed it. Why couldn't I remember?" questioned Sam.

There in the secret room was Colby, tied up in the middle of a pentagram. The walls covered in satanic symbols. Behind Colby Satan stood. Sam screamed, "Don't hurt him!"

Ellie Merrick (16)

Lost

Darkness surrounded me. I could barely see anything. Trapped Inside a basement, I reluctantly traversed towards the exit. Suddenly, light bulbs started to flicker. Fear captured me; I made out a glimpse of other people who had gone missing. My heart skipped a beat. It had been two days of redundantly laying here. The corpses were lifelessly staring at me. Instinctively, I dashed out of the entrance. It was there. A silhouetted figure lurking in the shadows. Without any regret, I hasted out of the house; outside was a dimly-lit road. Relief gradually conquered me. Fear destroyed relief. Lost.

Lucas Ong (12)

YoungWriters

Underground

Lost. Misplaced. Dead. Never to be found again... Ever
wondered why you could never find that missing pair of
socks? Or where the boy who lived down the street in the
derelict house went? Never to be seen again. When the
cover of night blankets them in darkness, they take without
mercy. Without prejudice. Dragging hopeless souls under
with them. Below. Thousands of feet underground, dingy
lighted tunnels run like a serpent crawling on the floor of an
endless desert. Intertwined like the cripple branches of a
tree. Chambers and chambers full of old trinkets and
damned beings. Forgotten about.

Rumi Begum (16)

Abandoned In Venice

Everything descended into oppressive darkness.

"Wait here," Dad had told me firmly. Venice had been majestic and haunting so far, with twisting canals dominating the city like serpents, juxtaposed next to the stunningly illuminated Rialto bridge.

He shouldn't be too long now surely. The toilets were only two minutes away...

Except, time for me had stopped. A sickening crack from the walls around me, a metallic stench from the street lights. As my terrorised mind crumbled in shock, I collapsed to the ground, slumped against stone. My heart thundering in my chest. Where was Dad?

Ishaan Harkhani (11)

Vanished

There once was a town like any other, beautiful, full of laughter, happiness and joy, where the sun shone rays of hope and purity, like a perfect paradise. But suddenly, everyone was gone, all vanished from existence. Never to feel the warm, bliss sensation of sunshine again. There was no investigation, their lives were forever lost in the secrets of time. Some believe they still lurk in the shadows, hiding from whatever demons that frightened them away. However, I guess we will never really know. But wherever they were and whatever they did, why they disappeared, will be forgotten forever.

Maddie Davis (11)

Missing

I was charging, running down the battlefield when I heard the unmistakeable purring of a V1 rocket soaring overhead, the explosion's shockwave dismembering many soldiers. I lost a hand. "My hand!" I screamed. Tears of pain running down my face... 'MIA', they said - missing in action. I'm presumed dead to many, I was replaced like I was expendable. I wanted vengeance. I gave myself into the Germans, I let the torture happen. I wanted my commander and my leader, everyone dead, everyone who replaced me dead to my blade. "Ha, ha, ha!" I laughed maniacally...

Alec Lothian (13)

A Blind Scavenger

The door creaked open, the nurse stepped in.
"Sorry dear, no one has come to visit you for three years,
neither have you woken up." Distressed, she sat on my bed.
"Your eyes remind me of my daughter, Lyra. She had those
emerald eyes, one that went missing one summer morning,
twenty years ago and... never came back."
Wiping away a tear, her hand reached the red button.
"Noooooooooo!" I cried but she never heard me and never
would. "Mum, it's me. Your Lyra."
With those last words, my world became dark.
Missing things are often in front of us.

Jaria Mirza (15)

Into The Forest

I'm running. My feet are hurting, but I won't stop. Not until I am away from that monster. That traitor. That... That... No words can even describe that 'thing'. No words can describe the hatred I am feeling right now. I'm fast approaching a forest. It doesn't look very welcoming. Perfect. No one will look for me here. Finally. Freedom. Lights blind me. There's a squeal of brakes. Darkness. Silence.
I try to get up. I can't... I try to move. I can't... I try to call out. I can't... I'm trapped. I wanted to be missing, instead I'm found.

Sophie Partridge (12)

Miss Sing

Her fingers caressed the rigid wall, jamming them up with splinters as she tried reaching the light's warmth through the cracks. Singing was the island to which she could reach the sky and herself, by which she retained herself from drifting away into the abysmal darkness surrounding her at present.

Harsh cold. The night at last arrived, she begged the light to stay as she didn't want it to leave again. Her heartbeat, smoke-stained, danced along to her guitar like it used to. Her body deposited under where he slumbered, without a promising sign of profound peace she said goodbye.

Kristina Manolova (17)

The Mystery Of The Missing Relics

Crash! Suddenly Jackson's heart started to pound against his newly pressed security jacket. "I knew it, this isn't for me at all!" he muttered not to be detected. There were no other candidates to take the job after the history of disappearing relics in this museum. Jackson, who is extremely skinny and petite, sprinted down the main staircase in terror trying to catch the thief when he spotted priceless paintings and valuable statues of historic people missing. Jackson reached for his radio but it was too late. He had come face-to-face with... "Argh!"

Oliver Swales (12)

The Runaway

I was right there when it happened. The day Emily Moore went missing. Search parties were strewn across the country in order to find her, with no luck. Policemen swarmed around the suspects, witnesses and the so-called parents like bees, scanning everyone for any visible traits of uncertainty, or deceit. As I watched it happen, I couldn't help but notice the strained look on the parent's faces, a fake sense of nurturing painted on their bleak pale faces, their tired eyes outlined in multiple dark circles. Yet all this defeated the purpose of why I decided to disappear one night.

Julia Okon (13)

SOS SAGAS: MISSING - TALES FROM THE UK

The Replacement

I wish I could stop running and give myself up, just to find some peace. But it was dark and claustrophobic underneath the floorboards. I only just managed to claw myself out. If she finds me, then I'm as good as dead.

I don't know who *she* is but I've reached my home. It doesn't matter anymore. They must be so worried; I peer through the window. Why does everything look... normal? I hear laughter, I see... myself inside. It's like looking in a mirror. Except, she's smiling back.

And then it hits me. I'm not missing.

I've been replaced.

Alisha Khan (17)

Missing

Glaring up into the cold, lifeless sky, the girl's breathing quivered. Her expression was blank like a slate wiped clean of the knowledge it once possessed. She was scared; fear wrapping around her insidiously, taking hold of her vulnerability.

Questions warred within her mind: who was she? Where was she? In many ways, why was she? She violently shook her head, such questions distorted what little she knew. But she looked up, that dark sky. It was empty, like something had gone. She wept knowing that reality would never give her the answers to the questions she asked. *Why?*

Kit Parsons (14)

A Missing Cure

A blood-curdling scream echoed through the silence of the house. The wind howled with its obstinate mocking, rattling floorboards. The monster of a house loomed over the isolated streets, only serving as a home to a deranged scientist. Working constantly, his lab was his life driving him forward with determination. If nobody could find a cure for the mutating virus sweeping the globe, he would. His stomach churned and thick acid scored his throat. Nobody was there to hear his scream. He reached for his most prized possession but his hands were met with cold air. The cure was missing...

Samara Natania Korapaty

Missing

Missing. The object that had saved lives and could still is missing, I thought as I peered into the blank and empty bag, stinging with hope that my eyes deceived me. What was missing of course was the xequacord, which acquires the capabilities to communicate peacefully to beings on other planets. Lives will be lost. Misunderstandings will sprout. Wars will rage. All because I lost some silly toy. I glared around the room, aiming to identify the thief. But the problem was there were so many mischievous faces in the class it was almost impossible to decipher who was responsible.

Hector Ghikas (12)

The Last Mistake

It was an ordinary day in Britain until the clock struck 4:30 on June 20th 2023. Out of nowhere several men pulled out guns, yelling and swearing, during the Prime Minister's press conference. Shots went off killing four bodyguards risking their lives, while the fifth didn't move. Faster than the speed of light a mask was brought over the Prime Minister's head and the criminals made an easy getaway with all witnesses murdered.

June 20th 2024: "We will not make the same mistake losing the life of a great prime minister, but will ensure the safety of the next one."

Liam Hughes (13)

Missing

The ransom note arrived. I watched my mother's fingers tremble, her eyes scanning the page. "One million pounds..." Her voice was barely a whisper. She read and reread the note, as if that would somehow bring back my sister, her only daughter. I watched her rock back and forth, tears streaming down her face. I watched as she assured me that everything would work out, my sister wouldn't die. I watched her blame herself repeatedly, and I regretted what I'd done. Guilt piled upon my shoulders like a burden - my sister wasn't missing. She was dead. Because of me!

Debbie Afolayan (13)

With The Stranger

'Missing!' The text glared at me, daring me to question it. They used a photo she hated, always annoyed by the lighting. I just focused on her eyes, falling into the sparkling blue once again. My own eyes had wet rings beneath them, formed the moment I heard their report. "... Seen two days ago... Hagley Wood..." Forced to find out like an ordinary person - as if I wasn't her girlfriend. I don't know why. That wasn't my biggest question. That would be why she had appeared ten minutes earlier, eyes foggy, mumbling a greeting before heading to the shower.

Amman Ahmed (16)

Train Ride

Dear Diary,
I'm on the train. It's been an hour since I ran away and my mother seems not to have noticed. She hasn't called or texted me. I don't think she cares. Father's worried, he's called many times but if I answer I will regret my decision. The urge to turn around would overpower me and who knows what would happen then. I'll write when I arrive. I can't say where I am going in case this is read.
Goodbye,
Melanie.

No more entries have been recorded. Melanie was never found. Washington State police department. Monday, January 12th 2015.

Keisha Lehrle (12)

England's Secret Service

Welcome to the British boot camp, where we train Britain's finest agents. If you're reading this it means your child has been selected. Congratulations! Now you have to sign a legal document explaining that you must go to the police and file a missing person's report and you'll get £100,00 for letting us draft him. If you do not then we will send trained men to assassinate you. As sad as this is to do to innocent families like you, unfortunately, it must be done. I do hope you're not too upset. Remember, it's for our country!
Yours sincerely,
MI6.

Tyler Sebestyen (14)

Missing In Action

The darkened plane flew low; the ground rushing past; wild eyes within darting around - searching the environment. Swinging the Focke-Wulf Fw190 around, the aviator cast his eye over the horizon seeking tell-tale signs of a crash: smoke, fire, impact marks... anything.

Making one final pass, the pilot abandoned his fateful search - British forces were closing in. He would have to break the news to the family. It was the least he could do for his best friend.

The plane set off for Germany, over the Dover cliffs. Behind him a single plume of smoke curled into the sky.

Abbey Jones (13)

Wave Of Guilt

The music frizzled and crackled through the air like electricity, the vibrations travelled through her body, as she floated towards the beach. Detective Kiyo sipped the coconut water as his eyes followed her; the girl that decided to disappear. Nobody noticed, the sniper as it fired a soundless shot that shook her body as it crumbled into the ocean. 'Jigou jitoku - you get what you deserve!' Smirking he returned the silencer. His Casio winked in the teasing sunlight, as he took another sip and the tick-tock of time drowned out the truth. No longer was his daughter missing.

Celestin James (17)

Silence

I set to work, etching the answers to the equations on my whiteboard. From the hallway, silence poured into the maths classroom, leaving only Miss Bark's fingers tapping on keys at high speed preventing ultimate silence, along with the quiet squeak of my whiteboard pen.

When I finally finished my task, I peered across the silent classroom and noticed a slight difference. I decided to raise my hand to ask. The teacher peered up over the rim of her glasses at my outstretched arm. "Yes, Tim?"

"Miss, where are the other students?" I asked from my empty desk...

Freya Lynn Perry (14)

Devoid

I was surrounded by it. Darkness. Silence. Nothing. I was turning, staring in all directions, my heart pounding and my breath increasing. As I stared into the emptiness, I reached out in hope there'd be something for my shaking palms to latch onto. Nothing. I stumbled around aimlessly trying to find something... anything within the darkness. My eyes began watering as I panicked more, blurring my already unseeing eyes. I didn't know where I was, or how I got here. I ran into the emptiness of the void ahead; everything was missing, including my own senses... or maybe I was.

Shannon Lane (16)

A Deadly Vaccination

I prayed that after the vaccination, everything would return to normal. I paused, then pushed the school doors open. The dread I had carefully hidden within my thoughts now screamed at me to turn back, like a burning weight sinking into my shoulders, the fear energising and powerful. I entered. All I could grasp was the lifeless expressions carved on their faces; the children could barely smile, eyes bleak. Snapshots of how broken they appeared played repeatedly in my mind. Fragments of identity shattered as if it had been pulled out of them. So why hadn't it affected me yet?

Isabel Michaelis (14)

Missing

It's now missing. Police notified, guards on the lookout. The palace never seemed so threatening. Stone walls bounding over my actions, cold; like the wine cellar storage room. It inflicted fear into my heart, an emotion worse than something so primitive as pain. A flow of electrical currents course through my body, adrenaline kicking in, panicking is not a stage I want to reach. I creep round the circular base of the pillars and jump into the sewers but not before sounds of heavy thumping feet arrive above the drainage cover. Three words spring to mind: *hide or run?*

Nathan Bird (15)

Fate

I woke up one morning, not knowing what time it was. I looked around and realised it wasn't my room! As I panicked and trembled, I looked around the room and found a newspaper... it was me. It read: 'Missing, if not found in 48 hours then presumed dead'. *They'll never find me*, I thought whilst wiping my tears and opening the door. It's locked... Just then through the window a bright light shone. From the blacked-out window, I just about managed to see people... Deep inside I knew one of them. "Father, here upstairs!" I said. Was my end near?

Ruchi Goel (11)

22nd June

If you know what the effect of so-called 'black swan' is, you might already assume what will happen in here.

It was a peaceful, benevolent, bright day of June 1941. Misha, with his friends, found something curious, he was holding something full of dust and mud, this was an old, deteriorate crocodile toy. "I'll bring him home, I will clean him and we will become friends and have a happy future together."

Morning 22nd was sore, the malevolent noise of blades was heard everywhere, now we can understand that the day of extreme climax arrived.

The war started...

Victoria Ciugainova (16)

A COVID Operation

Jonesy is the name, private eye is the game! Reports of toiletries; shampoo and hand soap disappearing into the unknown. Toilet roll? Did it ever exist or has it gone missing? Investigation commenced, I will leave no sheet unturned, following each roll for clues.

Breaking news, reports of a toilet roll creature that is crunching through the lot. We must find it, defeat it and return toilet roll to every bathroom in the nation.

I know what this is... COVID-19.

Closing in on me, deadly pressure on my chest, struggling to draw breath... Sacrificing life to restore world normality.

Oliver Baker (12)

Fallen Kingdom

Every step they take, they befoul the place... Every look they take, they bring nothing but desolation... Within their fingertips, they hold our death, glistening in the golden sun... From the sky, I gaze down upon them, watching them unleash their dark powers on our beloved kingdom. Forevermore, we are at their mercy as they destroy our realm. With what they possess in their hands, they take us away, one by one, stealing fragments of our kingdom's soul. Bits of my heart disintegrates as I glide through the sky, doing nothing but watch helplessly as the humans take us away.

Tahmid Ibrahim Chowdhury (13)

Missing

My hand brushed briefly over the surface of my pocket, the soft, slightly squishy, synthetic cotton folding and warping as it responded to my touch. An amalgamation of panic and terror struck and ruptured every ounce of my being. Countless thoughts rushed through my brain, each a scenario of the implications caused by what I had. In my pocket, was absence, the absence of a phone. Within seconds I found myself frantically scanning the area, every clump of foliage and tuft of grass became victim to a glare of anxious frenzy. My attention turned towards a drain beside my feet...

Luke David Baillie (15)

Gone

"Ma'am, I'm sorry to say your husband is missing," consoled the police officer in a soft tone.

"My husband is what?" I asked in a distressed tone, hoping to sound devastated, maybe hysterical.

"I will leave you to mourn."

Shame, I thought as he left. *Such a catch.* But I had a bigger problem, what to do with my husband? In the world's eye he's missing, in mine he's dead. Yet I couldn't get paid with him found dead. Next time I'm married he will be older. I loved him but I loved his money so much more.

Genabou Boiro

Launched

My grimy prison bars approach... no... not again. My whiskers scan the fumbling hand. My mouth encloses warm flesh. The ground is flung away. Fur whips back and ears fight sudden pressure; I zoom out the window. The scream fades. Shivering, I glance around. Clouds hang in the sky, darkening other nearby roofs. My bones chilled, I tumble down rough bumps on sore paws. I hover at an edge. A gust toys with me. I drop. Huge cage bars. Blackness. I awake in mountainous bedding. A monster of fur grunts beside me. A stranger's voice, "Mummy! Cheese Puff has babies!"

Amelie Cook (12)

Wax Museum

They're out there, scrutinising me. What do they want? I see a silhouette. Skin tones glisten in the moonlight. I hear murmurs and the reverberation of footsteps. Watched continuously and yet afraid of being alone, you'd think I'd be used to it by now.

A turn of his head in my direction! Is he human? Terror surges through me with each breath, settling on my skin like a dark fog. His fixed smile distorted. I'm drenched in sweat, as he's dragged towards me, positioned amongst other waxworks. Wait - he winks as I catch his demonic stare. Is he a waxwork?

Priyanka Harkhani (12)

Missing

There I am. A mugshot of me wrapped tightly around a lamp post, with the word: 'MISSING' in bold letters underneath. However, that's not what catches my attention, rather the way they describe me. It forces me to think, *am I wanted or missing?* You could say my actions were criminal - I don't feel like one because most criminals are careless and stupid. I had planned this for years, every step. I'm feeling good, which is strange considering my actions could send me down for life. But I know where I'm heading and I know what I have with me!

Ella Reeves (15)

The Unreliable Teleporter

One day, I found myself opening the cellar door. We were cautioned about the dilapidated, eroded house but I knew it was hiding a secret. Struggling not to cough as grimy dust tumbled down, I noticed a few books arranged haphazardly. I took a hesitant step forward onto a ramshackle platform as it shook uncontrollably.

The next thing I recall doing was waking up on damp sand. I was wearing the same clothes as before and the destination seemed completed desolate. That was when I considered myself to be permanently lost. I wonder if I really will be lost forever...

Vasilina-Natalie Kutsinova (12)

Gone Missing

It was a late Sunday night on a sandy beach. Everything was in the shadows or covered by dark clouds, a storm was brewing. It wasn't safe. Families darted off the beach leaving behind any unnecessary items. This storm came so sudden. Everyone was gone apart from one individual, one brave soul not scared of the sharp winds and rain. All of a sudden, there was a crash. A deafening crash of thunder followed by a blinding spike of lightning. After that it was silent. Families witnessed everything going back to normal, but that one individual had gone. Gone missing...

Lilia Dorman (14)

Soulless

Staring at me was a ghastly monster with gnarled ebony vines seeping across its face, defined against its sallow skin. Yet that monster was my reflection.

The soul snatchers have stolen everything. Now, I was only a shard of what I once was. An ocean of misery crashed through my body, waves of despair lapping at my heart. Lungs. Head. The meadow that once housed my soul lay in smouldering ruins. I am cracked. Empty. Lifeless. I might as well be dead. Soulless - was this what it felt like? Everything forced from me. Missing. The soul snatchers will regret everything.

Jessica Huang (15)

Without A Trace

The phone rang continuously. Every call was the report of another missing person. At the end of her shift, Abigail had 57 cases of people who had all vanished. No one had ever experienced this kind of predicament before, the whole city was panicked. The rate of missing people had accumulated from 4 to 140 in two weeks and was showing no sign of decreasing.

The FBI headquarters was filled with agents trying to make sense of the mysterious happenings. They were so focused on trying to find the missing, they didn't notice when one of their own vanished... Abigail!

Ruth Samuel (11)

Lost And Lifeless

The overwhelming darkness of the house and muffled screams from underneath the floorboards. K's footsteps echoed throughout the barren rooms, her urge to continue faltering at every step, the tick of the clock racing forward. She crawled up the stairs to what appeared to be a dusty attic. Her hand gripping a rusty handle in the middle, she tugged. It opened. And there she was. Lying in a heap, lifeless and still. Emily was missing all these years but she was here. Dead. In the reflection of her glasses, a shadow loomed over her, and this shadow held a blade...

Milla Shuttleworth (13)

Abandoned

Her scent still fresh, like she was still here. I inhaled again, desperate to smell something, but it was just her perfume that lingered in the air. She had never left me before. My mouth opening wide, desperately trying to alert her; my barks echoing around the room, only to come rushing back to my ears. I didn't stop, I couldn't. I needed someone to come, anyone. My owner gone, missing. I was abandoned. A rush of footsteps approached, a head appeared, eyes bulging. Leaping up onto the windowsill, peering down I saw why. She lay in the grass. Motionless.

Claire Aiken (14)

The Escape

The ransom note arrived through the door. I reached for the scruffy, crumpled note. 'DO NOT RUN'. My heart, thumping like a boulder was hitting me. I was kidnapped!
Realising that I had my pocket knife, I took out the sharp blade. I was released! I found a door; thick, heavy chains and a lock choked the door handle. Ruffling my hazelnut hair, I found a pin to help me. *Thump!* The chains fell, like I couldn't breathe. I was screaming air. They were coming with their metal poles. *Bang.* He was coming. My thirteen years were over...

Viththaky Sureskumar (12)

Curiosity

There was a boy named Joseph, he was living a simple life, until one that day all changed. Until then Joseph had never had any problems at school, but one day he came in differently than usual. He would normally greet everyone, and usually have a good attitude, but he never spoke to anyone that day.

The next day he didn't even come in. Everyone thought maybe something had happened to him, and the teachers thought that something had occurred. Soon there were missing posters hanging around the borough, but no one ever found him. Why did he just disappear?

Kristiyan Ganev (13)

Lost In Bangkok

Alex was missing, lost in Bangkok. Whenever he asked for a sip of water he was swatted away like a fly. Thoughts raced through his mind. When were the police going to find him? He kicked a stone and there he stood, an old foe.
"We meet again," he spat. His pungent smell filled the air. Alex shuddered. "Here we go again," he muttered.
Alex turned around, only now did he realise how big the ship was. "Please find me!" and as he said that a helicopter arrived. "Yes!" he cried... No, wait, it was his parents...

Ayeyi Asante (11)

These Wings Weren't Made To Fly

Part of me was missing, my wing. Where was the happy girl in the picture? Where was the little girl who made daisy chains every Saturday morning? Ever since I came out to my parents, none of us have been the same. Of course, Dad kicked me out, called me an embarrassment and Mum had 'lost her Princess', because I wasn't her 'Princess' anymore, I was her 'Prince'. They had lost their little girl, the one who painted her nails pink, used Mum's make-up, played dress-up and wore her fairy wings. The wing snapped, and I no longer flew.

Megan Groza (14)

Lucifer's World

After being excluded from Heaven, Lucifer made his own world, a world for sinners. A world of fun and laughter. A world called Hell. I had led an unfortunate life free of sins, so I was sent to Heaven.

God is throwing a very boring, sin-free party. I am trying to find a way to get away from here, to get sent to Hell. With the salad bowl in my hands and God's halo, his back towards me, a plan comes to mind.

I blink and am greeted by a crying-laughing-on-the-floor Lucifer Morningstar.

"Welcome," he says. "We've been missing you."

Louise-Paige Chapman (13)

Hell's Gates

She's missing. It felt eerie. The news had left us shell-shocked and had created a deep dent in our now metallic hearts. The sinews tugging our lifeline together were torn apart by the whetted blades of a tiger at a lamb.

Days and nights shifted by silently, creeping at a snail's pace with the stealth of a snake. Every night, I'd peer up towards hell's gates, the menacing screen swallowing up all sense of balance.

Like a shot, lightning cracked above, striking the pang. A thousand pins rip my wound open. I'm a caged bird. In an absent sky.

Tushita Gupta (13)

Hope

Amongst the sirens, the grief and the debris, nothing seemed so alien until he fell. On his knees. Face first. In the dirt. I had been surviving on the bare minimum and doubted I could do nothing more than breathe. He had found hope amongst this war zone when I couldn't. The world was falling apart but there was something intact; us. I was too late. I helplessly held on to him and whispered, "Don't leave me." His body went limp.

I shot him dead. Another ran but was too late. He whispered, "Don't leave." His body went limp.

Hena Afridi (15)

Captive

I grimaced as rope scratched at my skin, clutching to a desperate memory of home, an impossible hope of freedom. I did not know how long had passed, it seemed that the barren room would be my deathbed; the metal bars my last sight of daylight, of everything they had taken from me. Suddenly, the soft thud of footsteps consumed the silence, then the whispers came, followed by shouting coming from downstairs. This wasn't those who imprisoned me, it couldn't be, could it? The door was wrenched open and I saw a hazy silhouette before everything went black.

Lucas Nijhof-Clarke (12)

Familiar Faces

Yours was the first face I couldn't remember. It was so familiar yet so distant, it scared me. I ransacked my memories, searching for any remnants of who you once were. It appeared that all those joyous laughs and bright smiles were now missing; replaced by scars that etched themselves deep into your newly sallowed, jaundiced skin. To think there was a time where you looked at me as though I were beautiful, now the only lingering expression in your eyes is predatory, sinister. I lowered my gaze, accepting my fate - the person I loved is now forever gone.

Sarra Mhiri (17)

Missing

Ping! The lead snapped and Stan was off like a rocket, disappearing over a stone wall, startled by the roar of a winged beast. The girls chased but Stan was gone, missing! But more worrying was that the weather had started to change, the sky grew grey and rain began falling. As the family tried to battle the weather a mist surrounded them and consumed the stone walls. As the family huddled together another ear-piercing screech boomed overhead, then out of the mist a man appeared with Stan cradled in his arms, as another fighter jet boomed overhead.

Katie Bailey (12)

An Old China Doll

It was on the news again. Another missing person, no leads, just gone.

It was dark outside, and Jessie was going home from work. It started pouring so she entered a shop she'd never noticed before. It was falling apart, but gothic and elegant. In the shop window Jessie saw an old china doll. It was staring at the street outside, while reaching out for something. Jessie impulsively picked it up and looked into its eyes. Before she realised it, she was behind glass, looking out into the street, stiff and unmoving, reaching out.

It was on the news again.

Aseda Adusei

One Year Later

Claire screamed and disappeared.

One year later, my hair stood on end, a shiver raced down my spine and a lump came to my throat. I breathed in and out but air wouldn't enter my lungs. My heart raced at a tremendous speed and I stood there for what felt like an eternity, actually it was only five minutes. It was Claire, but she was supposed to be dead, wasn't she?

"Amanda, I know how confusing this must be but I'm trapped and you have to free me in twenty-four hours or I will be trapped forever." Claire sighed hopelessly...

Valentina Innamorati (13)

Disappeared Or Abducted?

Hi. I am a spy. Another two more years until I am finished with this mission, well I think. We are about to destroy their main servers and ruin their plan on using enough ultraviolet rays to build a destructive light to end us all. They rival us to the most powerful country in the world. I discovered something else while going through the president's drawer. I found the location of where our leading scientists are being held. I took a picture of it. "Hey, president's advisor, what are you doing?" Oh man, on my sixteenth birthday as well.

Syaam Hussain (12)

NHS Nurse Missing From Home

Bright, honeycomb-yellow beams of light pierced through the blackout curtains. My room blazed a multitude of magnificent colours of red and amber. I woke to the sound of silence. I searched the house and, to my surprise, I was accompanied only by specks of dust that sat peacefully on the old picture frames. Many thoughts flourished through my mind. I repeated the thought my mom was missing. I ran to the door to find it wasn't locked. Silence filled the house as I wondered whether I was dreaming. Sullen silence for the rest of my life? Will she return?

Cole Carrick (13)

Free

I ran rapidly through the woods; the wind and the rain argued loudly. The cold crisp rain drenched me as I heard the satisfying sound of red autumn leaves crunch behind me. Running deeper into the forest the trees were joined together like a crowd of vivid green umbrellas sheltering me from the pelting rain; suddenly a smoky scent of wood-fire shifted to my nose. My emotions were on fire and flashbacks of trauma and torture flooded my confused brain. I shook the memories of violence out of my confused brain and thought of a plan: escape and find shelter.

Ramani Mattu (13)

The Unsolved Mysteries

They were last seen in March 2001. The disappearances still remain a mystery. Clues had been left around the area of those missing, however, investigators have not yet found out what happened. Until 2020, a mountain walker came across a weathered locket chain. Curious, he opened it. What he didn't know is that this was a vital piece to the puzzle. Inside, a folded up piece of paper gave coordinates to what would soon be revealed as the grave of a Miss Rogers, missing since 2001! Who killed her? Who will be found next? This still remains a mystery...

Maddison Arscott (12)

Perfect Fake Facade

If you looked at me you would see a blonde-haired girl with red Converse and always wearing a big smile. You probably would think I'm the happiest person alive. But, have you ever heard of 'don't judge the book by its cover'? Well, I'm its perfect example. I'm a broken girl with a perfect fake facade to cover her demons. Even if you knew me seven months ago, when my world still hadn't fallen apart, you wouldn't have realised that I'm not the same anymore and that I just know how to act as if I hadn't lost my soul.

Geovana Maziero Camarotto (13)

Erased From Existence

I pried my eyes open and awoke, after an eternity of battling against the dark void which encompassed me within my mind. And after enduring the weight of fear and loneliness I have freed myself from my mental prison, only to be greatly disappointed to find myself once again trapped by darkness. I was unfamiliar with my surroundings and could only identify vivid shadows and a dim source of light, seemed infinitely far away from my grasp. Yet the greatest mystery posed upon me was the feeling of emptiness within me. My name, my age, who I am, was missing.

Kamil Szakiel (15)

Him

She woke up in a crystalline cage. Her breath caught in her throat. Suffocation. Her body felt burdened with heavy, murky mist shrouding her thoughts. She could feel a thick, heavy liquid seeping down her face. The memories instantaneously came flooding back, running in circles. Blocking her mind. She remembered his heavenly face and loving eyes. In times of great uncertainty, she would assure herself by making a list of all that she knew; she knew she was missing and she knew she had to find him. She heard the lock of the cage door opening. She ran...

Hannah Lynch

Where Did It Go?

The money was missing, there was nothing left to do. I had to find the kleptomaniac who had taken all the money from the safe. I had spent months collecting nine thousand, nine hundred and ninety-eight pounds. I was exasperated. I don't remember myself leaving the safe opened or closed. I felt as if I was solving a puzzle with over a thousand pieces, it was arduous to figure out. Unfortunately, there were no traces of evidence to prove that someone had stolen my money. Things weren't making sense but I knew something was wrong. Where did it go?

Fatima Iftikhar (13)

The End Is Near

They'll never find me. I will never find me. Part of me has been missing ever since that irreversible nightmare. My life shattered like a crystal, within seconds. Ten dreaded years I have been searching for the missing piece, wondering if I will ever be found. Sitting in an isolated frosty tree looking down on what little life I have left. My tears fall faster than the waterfalls I pass. But yet I still drag myself onwards with the tiniest pinch of hope buried in my cold, dark heart. They'll never find me. I will never find me. I'm missing!

Molly Godfrey (13)

Concealed By The Darkness

Dream or nightmare? Waiting on something that has no return. Controlled like puppets on a string, left leg, right leg, right arm, left arm. Simply no one believes me. Who would? An orphan killing her own father. They know the truth, as do I. Blinded. Like all the others. Feeding on lies. Brainwashing every last one. Stealing him from me, tearing my heart piece by piece. Enter and you never leave. I will finish this puzzle if it's the last thing I do. Where do missing things really go? Do they ever return from the darkness or are they lost forever?

Shana-Leigh Fellows (15)

Shattered Glass

A hole in the window. I leave for seconds and there it is. Part of it missing. Okay, not missing, considering it was there on the floor, but missing from the window, yes - tomato, tomato. The shards seemed like gleaming crystal catacombs that danced in sunlight sharply. But concentrate - why a hole? Huh, the top of it looked awfully like a head - round, squashed. Come to think of it, below was something like a body - large, and mocking me with superior masculinity. But the hole - oh, I get it now! Someone jumped through! Someone must be in my... damn.

Sushant Shyam (13)

Bio War

The hard drive wasn't in the safe. The lab had been broken into in the night. If Doctor Roosevelt didn't find it, the world would be at risk. The hard drive contained the genetical information from the bio wars happening recently. More than one million people died from them and it shook the world's economy. He had found out that terrorists made these viruses, and no one knew. But Roosevelt had a trick up his sleeve, a solar-powered tracker was on the drive. He told the police the location and in three days, he had received the hard drive.

Arnav Kasireddy (12)

Forgotten

"Raissa? Huh? Raissa! Where are you? Hello! I'm here!" She's gone. Getting up on my feet, I analyse the damp footpath blanketed in moss. No beginning, no end, just one middle - or so it seems. My head suddenly throbs and I reach out for the stone-cold brick wall, suddenly tripping over a body. I freeze. It was my body. My lifeless body with its glassy nonchalant eyes gazing back at me. No one remembers who I am, that's probably how I came here. If only I could be found again. Run. What? Run. Where? Run to anywhere but here...

Raissa Hirji (13)

SOS Sagas Missing

The building towered over me. My breath enhanced rapidly, stomach churning and nails digging into my palms. Sweat dripped down my forehead. This was once a place of beauty and imagination. These cold windows formerly a warm home. The vast empty halls used to be brimmed with loving children. Once polished and shiny floors now tarnished and old. My sister being one of the loving children. Lost in the ghost stories of this mansion. I tried running but my feet were stuck to the ground. I tried to shout but when I opened my mouth all words escaped me.

Sanyia Choudhury (12)

Missing In Silence

Where the shadows were blocked and the doors were locked, was a town known as Horniph. The town was filled with these beasts known to be silenters. They could not see but if you were heard you wouldn't see the daylight again. One evening, a family decided to face the town's fear and adventure past their gates. The family had a little boy with them, his name was Gorgy. As they passed the shops, Gorgy begged to go in, so they went in but the item the boy wanted made a noise! *Zoom!* "The silenters!"
"Gorgy!"

Deanna Jebouri (12)

The Missing Spaniard

It happened so fast - the Spanish cockroach swam for his life to keep up with his friends in the swamped drains of New York. The storm had flushed the insects away, down a waterfall of rain and sludge into the sewage system of the disgusting city they called home. Roach-io could not swim fast enough, and he was soon abandoned by his loved ones in the damp darkness. They will never find him again, or even attempt to search - he was missing, presumed dead in the maze of grime, slime, and pollution. Roach-io began to cry, "Odio la vida."

Katie Bartlett

I Need To Stay Missing

My dreams were the only place I could escape, the only place I wasn't forgetting. The memories came back, playing over and over, as if I was watching a movie about myself. Slowly cloaking my senses, from that first meeting underneath the viaduct, I had started losing pieces of myself. Pieces I could never get back, pieces that made me who I am. A face haunted my dreams, with almond eyes, ringed with gold, stark in the moonlight. People would start looking for me, but I was becoming a stranger to myself and it was better if I stayed missing.

Evie McIntosh (13)

All Alone

The night was a blur as the girl was taken away into darkness which found her hours later. Unaware of anything, she started screaming for help, only to hear her own echo reply. Stumbling as she rose up to see the outside out the decade-old looking window to see that she was in an abandoned city with no movement. Within seconds, darkness appeared into the sky, even though it was still daytime. Lights of fire surrounded the city, with many helicopters of some kind she hadn't seen before, but little did she know this was only the beginning...

Gergana Manolova (15)

Lost

I awoke in a jet-black surrounding and heard an ear-bleeding sound from the monstrous rats rushing beneath my feet. Suddenly a sense of adrenalin and panic overpowered my body like 1000 volts of electricity, causing my body to frantically shake, revealing that I am bound to an ancient chair. I try to loosen the binds, but it just creates an agonising burning sensation to my weakened vulnerable wrists. Suddenly I dart from my bed screaming, a cold sweat dripping down my forehead, realising this spine-chilling experience was just a cruel dream.

Evan Palmer (12)

The Void

After all these years I finally found it. The place where lost souls are taken. I stand on the ledge looking down on them. I can hear a cacophony of misery. Wails, screams, the words of people accepted by no one. Thousands upon thousands of souls that no one wanted. Taken here by the governments of the world to solve all their problems. Famine, disease, mental health issues. I take a deep breath. "It's okay," I tell myself. "I've found them, the question is how on earth do I rescue them? How do I get them out...?"

Serena Cooper (14)

Alone In A Rainforest?

The unsettling scent of jet fuel and burning bodies circulated around the dense rainforest. He was the last one standing. The others had either been chargrilled or taken away by ravenous beasts. At last, there was a glimpse of hope: a low purr of a helicopter high above. However it was nothing to dwell upon, he would never be found. Suddenly a spear landed next to his foot like a dubious javelin. He slowly creaked his neck around... Before he got a glimpse, he passed out. The devil was going to claim his life. He was missing in a rainforest.

Jordan Giannasi

Untenable Thirst

When the drought had choked the cattle, guzzled up all the poultry, with their scaled and trident feet, rattled the figs from the leafless orchard, my uncle steps out onto the seared yard with the family dog and his killing blade pressed against his fat thumb. His wife is at his heels in a fleeting white dress, meshing her feet into rotten pears, tempting the flies with the soft edges of exposed ankles. No, the children did not listen. They watch, gangling behind the shrunken window, wondering what could still bleed out on the road, howling?

Anya Trofimova

Hide-And-Seek

I woke up to the thick smell of blood. Lucy, Tommy and Alice... twisted and mangled beside me. The pure horror that struck my face, yanked out streaming tears. I felt a pain, ripping my heart out of my chest. I couldn't breathe... or think. Hide-and-seek? This was not hide-and-seek. This was a gruesome torture chamber cellar. My watch appeared as Monday but last, last I could remember was Friday. A twinge of searing pain ripped my scalp as a tried to get up. Then... the door creaked open. I scurried to the corner of the room. My dad...?

Evie Hodgson (14)

I'm Still The Same

Part of me was missing; ever since I came back from science camp, it's as if I was brainwashed. Whenever someone asked me a question I wouldn't respond, I'd just zone off into a world of my own. Whenever my parents asked what I wanted to eat or if I wanted to go shopping, I couldn't remember who they were or what they were saying. It's not as if I didn't know who they were, I just couldn't find the words to respond with. All I could say when someone asked what's wrong is, "I'm still the same..."

Arnesh Srivastava (12)

Missing

Jessica adored school, her favourite subject was science. She thought it would be a great idea to bring a bug into school. Later that day she snuck away from her mum to look for one. Fifteen minutes passed and Jessica's mum started to search the house for her. She looked all over but her bungalow was clean of her. The mother was panicking, she was taking deep breaths and going light-headed. While on Jessica's side of life there was no problems, or so it seemed. There was no sign of the bug but most importantly no sign... of home...

Max Pattison (12)

The Signal

It was 23:15, we waited for the signal. We were outside the heavily guarded police depot where we were going to steal drugs worth millions. However, we knew nothing, all we knew was where to go, and what to get. Me and the other lads created theories, the most popular one came from Wiggs who thought we were working for a bent copper. We got the signal! We opened one of the depots and jackpot! As we were searching through the drugs and shoving them in bags... *bang!* I turned around, my dad stood with blood dripping down his clothes.

Alexander Rate (13)

Lost

Wait. What? Where did it go - I only looked away for a short second?
Searching high and low, quickly losing hope; adrenaline surging through my panicked veins as I was frantically darting around the endless control centre, playing cat and mouse to find what I had misplaced.
It felt like I had searched an entire galaxy, but of course... I had. How was I going to tell the rest of the expectant crew that the planet we were supposedly going home to was missing? That I'd lost sight of where we were landing? That I had lost Planet Earth...?

Thaya Warren (16)

My Last Day

The once silent roads were now filled with lashes of anger, jeers but also fearful cries which echoed around me. The rapid sound of my heart beating enveloped my ears. Loneliness was like a vice on my heart; every jostle from careless strangers made my eyes brim deeper with tears. Every gulp of air I took turned into sobs as I tried to reassure myself that these breaths I took were not my last. Pain seared through my abdomen, leaving me to lie there acknowledging what the world had become and appreciate the idea of this day being my last.

Fenet Chemir (13)

Bury The Truth

'Missing, presumed dead' the article read. I couldn't handle the shame of what I did. 'A frantic search for the missing girl.' I had to run away. 'New evidence... case opened again.' I thought I got rid of it. It was a blur. These three years have been the worst. An endless run. My life, dark, with the absence of her light. That I took. It felt like an eternal punishment. Let me go back to the beginning. The one I loved the most went missing. The one I loved the most left me. The one I loved most abandoned me.

Baveena Selvanendam (13)

Lost In Space

The minute I woke up I knew something was wrong. I went and put some clothes on, and decided to courageously venture outside. When I opened the door, I was so shocked I almost passed out; I was in the middle of space. When I went to assist my family, I discovered they weren't there but their possessions were floating. When I opened the window, it was so quiet that I could hear my breathing but suddenly I started hearing an eerie ringing getting louder in my ears. I was so deluded that I jumped and said, "Goodbye my world."

Powlo Remice (12)

A Thorn In A Sea Of Petals

There was a noise, hushed, but still audible. I rose and stepped to the window, opening my room to the orange haze of the streetlamps. I was immediately drawn to him, tucked so hastily away from the dim pool of light. A mask hid his face, or was it shadow? He was out of place; a thorny rose in a pond of velvet lilies. My heart pounded. He stood at the window of the Greenes' house, a bungalow. Peering inside, he cracked open the window. Realisation swallowed me, that was little Erica's room. My hands shaking, I called the police.

Libby Rix (13)

The Smell Of A Crime

Something smelt fishy and it wasn't just the smell of the accident scene. But that was the problem, because I doubt it was any accident. No body remained. The crash must have been staged. Someone was in trouble. There is a story to be uncovered. I could still see the firemen searching through the wreckage hoping to find anything, but all that was left was my dad's ruined Polo scattered in debris. I could see a tear in my mum's eye but I knew that this crash was no accident and that my dad was involved in a terrible crime...

Delina Vithani (12)

The Journey Of Self-Discovery

I was here. Yet myself was somewhere my brain couldn't comprehend. Lost in the deepest trenches of my rapidly blinding mind. Whilst helping others, unknowingly I was gradually losing myself with the fake smile that was daily painted on my innocent face. It led me to question my own happiness and who I truly was. I was lost. Missing. I never knew who I was or what made me different. Who was I? The question that would lead me on a never-ending hunt that only I could do. A journey of self-discovery. Was I ready to face the ugly truth?

Tricia Currie (15)

Fruit Picking

A breath...
Your breath...
It falls upon your face, like warm snow, bringing a tingling sensation of life back into you. Finally, you're awake and nowhere.
You were upside down. Hung like a piece of cured meat, from a rope hooked to the ceiling.
The voice from the handset tells you to turn and run for light. You don't question him, and shaken, scamper along, trying to make sense of it all.
Of what?
The voice asks for your name - to keep you sane, ripe.
Ready for picking.
Forever missing.

Ganesh Mistry (15)

The Mysterious Space

During midnight, Marcus was moving house, the grumpy van driver sitting and waiting for Marcus to move his wardrobe into the van. He struggled to move his intensely heavy wardrobe. He grunted and moaned as he pushed it out the door. He was leaning on a doorknob he had never seen before. He got stunned in vast shock. He was intrigued to turn the knob. He made sure nobody was around, especially the mad van driver who was waiting for hours. He gently turned it and was shocked for what he had found. Marcus was never heard of ever again...

Armaan Raheel

An Escaping Inventor

One cold evening, as the darkness shrouded the sky, Sarah walked home whilst the words of the village's keeper replayed in her mind. If the inventor was her mother, if she was valued in the village, then why did she run away? The more she thought about it, the colder she got.

That evening, when she got home, she sat with her grandmother who she lived with, near the warm fireplace. She felt a pang of hatred for her grandma because she hadn't told her about her mother. No matter where she was Sarah was going to find her...

Rola Al-Hassani (11)

Thursday, 29th April

Every day was the same as the day before, until that one day when everything changed. I woke up excited for the day to begin.

Walking to school I passed the fifth house on the right, which always made me smile the most, as Old Edna usually sat in her garden waving away to my little sister and I, drinking her herbal tea. Thursday, 29th April changed everything. Her rocking chair was empty. No smile, no wave. Nothing.

Birds still chirp in nearby trees, the gate creaks but no sound comes from the empty porch. No sound at all.

Sophie Ryder (12)

The Stealth

The home of Raska Badneer was heavily guarded, armed soldiers patrolled the high fence. Raska was a millionaire, she earned a living off her dad's never-ending will, thousands of pounds trickled into her bank every second. She lay sleeping on her velvet sofa. Raska did not wake as the man disposed of her guards, silently taking care of them one by one, nor did she notice him climbing through her window; quiet like the summer breeze but cold-hearted like the winter chills. He drugged her and stealthily took her to places unknown.

Archie Lewis (11)

Lost In The Dark

Black. That is all I can see. I have been lost in the darkness for hours. Wandering aimlessly through the ebony sea with my location unknown. *Click!* The sound of a switch echoes through the shadows. Out of the corner of my eye, I can see a dim light not too far away. Blinded by the belief that somebody had come to find me, I ran straight towards the light. The closer I got, the brighter it became. Then the darkness returned. The sound of a sinister laugh echoed around me. This nightmare was not going to end anytime soon...

Hannah Jayne Bennett (14)

The Convenience Store

I was sickened by the whole situation. I sealed the VHS tape carefully. The address was already on the box. I felt my tense shoulders relax. Too much had happened in a short span. My mind couldn't keep up. I had to rest, but I couldn't fall asleep. What did I see? Was everything I witnessed even real? One comment on a strange forum stood out to me. I searched for the same user's comments in 2009 - three murdered. One body missing. The VHS tape - the person I saw - that was him. Suddenly, a loud knock came at the door...

Junior De Carvalho Rosa (12)

Gone!

Victor completed his class project and was proud of it. During the project presentation period, Victor came to the front of the class to present his work. He looked in his bag, but his project work was missing. He pleaded with his teacher for permission to look for it. Miss Smith gave him until 9am the next morning. Victor searched the whole school to no avail.

At home, his younger brother came to him. "Everyone in my school said your project is awesome," he explained, placing the project on the table in front of Victor.

Mofijinfoluwa Olayiwola (11)

Gone

The cold wind brushes against my skin as I try to slow my breathing down. I reach out my hands but instead of feeling the softness of my bedsheets, I am instead greeted by the rough texture of dry soil between my fingers. I slowly open my eyes and allow them to adjust to the darkness surrounding me. My heart speeds up. I'm outside. But why? I look around and see no sign of the house, the farm or even the town. Slowly, I lift myself up off the ground. A branch breaks from behind me...
"Finally, you're awake!"

Polychronia Maria Moschouris (15)

The Family

The family had been missing for two weeks. They left everything. The police had told everybody on the street, they questioned everybody too. Nobody knew what happened, their cars were still there, passports still in the drawers, it was as if they never existed. Everybody had their own theory. Some said that they were criminals on the run. Nobody liked them anyway, they were selfish and cruel, they killed a dog once. I could hear the stone drop on to the neck of the poor dog as I tried to sleep. I'm glad my dad did what he did.

Logan Wilson (14)

Forgot

Reluctantly I open my eyes expecting to see the dark empty room I've been seeing for years now, expecting to hear the TV rattling from downstairs. When my eyelids open all I can see is a blinding light that submerges me. All I can hear is the deafening sound of silence. I am neither dead nor alive. I am missing. I am forgotten. I don't know who I am, who I'm meant to be. I'm just a missing piece from a world that lives on communication, a world where forgetting and being forgotten is a pain far greater than death.

Coby Drew (13)

The Game Of Hide-And-Seek That Went Wrong

There was nothing. Nothing was left. My 'friends' told me to go hide and they would seek because of how good a hider I am. I was very impressed when after an hour they still hadn't found me but after two hours I began to question where they were. Maybe they were hurt? I should probably go check they were okay. I crept out from in-between the fridge and the cupboard where I was hiding and began to call out, "You've won, I give up," when I noticed my mom and dad's door was open and so was their safe...

Harry Martin (12)

SOS: Save Our Souls

Sprinting through the forest can keep you busy for a while. Especially when you're playing with your friend! I had lost track of time and Amy, my friend, decided it was time to go home. Time had rushed past and we hadn't even noticed. Only there was one problem. "I can't remember where to go..." I muttered, trying to focus. We tried to wander, seeing if it would get us anywhere. But we just ended up going in circles. So, this was really it. We couldn't find our home, anywhere. We gave up. We were lost...

Macie Real

Unexpected Goodbye

Missing, presumed dead, but I knew otherwise. I just needed to figure out where he was. I sat there trying to pin down where he could be, trying to find any possible reason why someone would want this.

I heard a noise. I ran over and there was a stomach-churning letter at my feet, demanding I pay £10,000. They must've known I was left everything in my father's will? I had never run so fast!

I bolted up to my attic, digging through box after box. But it was empty? I would never get to see my brother again.

Isla Ennis-Smillie

Missing

It's April 2020, the world's in lockdown. 'Missing' is a word used so often by so many. I miss my family during these strange times but most of all my rugby team. I feel lost without them in my life. We decided to compile a film of all my team throwing and receiving a ball from each other. This totally brightened up my day and made me smile.

The human race is being so creative and resilient right now. I'm proud to say even though we are facing dark times, it's great to see the world come together as one.

Cai Williams (11)

The Search

Where am I? Why can't I remember? The last memory I have is two weeks ago. I doubt that will help me. I seem to be in some sort of container, but it's too smooth to be metal. I hear voices outside the container; it seems to me that they are looking for someone. I see light as my container is opened. "We've got another one!" Then I feel a hand pull me up and put me back down again. "Nevermind, it's just a mannequin." I hear. What am I then? Then the memories came flooding back. I am trapped...

Jesper Fitzsimmons

Taken

The dead of night took over day, the moon appeared in its crescent shape and the tired sun sunk down until it was seen no more. They knew it was getting dark, time to go home, but they kept on going. Their shadows grew and darkened on the wall of the cave, crushing all light that tried to break in. A sharp intake of breath was heard from behind, along with the *CLANG!* of a lantern smashing into pieces, darkening the cave further. It was hard to see but surely one of them was gone. Taken, perhaps, but undeniably missing.

Aziza Khan

Utterly Alone

Sat in the window of an abandoned church. I look at the ghost of a hand on the side of the window. Someone has been here before. Hyper-vigilant. I fall into a darkness, trepidation spikes through my body. The darkness surrounds me and takes my breath. I try to call out, but the darkness intoxicates me. Numb. Motionless. Trying to look around, I see a light in the distance above me. I reach out but that once familiar light is hidden by the darkness with a shield of a thousand sorrows. I am utterly alone. I'll never be found.

Azaria Scott (15)

Orb Of Value

Hmph, you. Where is the Orb you promised me? You promised, dear, you would find my precious Orb. I'm a busy woman, I don't have time for delays or false wishes. My missing Orb will be found. You know why that orb is so valuable? Because that Orb contains the blood of 8000 men's souls turned to solid power. Now, you will find it, or you'll be the first soul of my next collection. However, I know you have it. Where is it? Fine. I'll get it myself, though I just loaded my flintlocks. *Pew, pew...*

Evelyn Kenrick (15)

Oblivion

I'm oblivious when it comes to you. The devilish thoughts of us being one cloud my mind and I melt to your touch. My innocence seems to evaporate when I'm around you. I see angel but they see demon. I see daydream but they see nightmare. My eyes were deceived with your perfect facade, only to finally uncover your ruins. I pictured my eternity to be with you, only to find out my eternity's distorted, just like you. The one I love is missing; he was never there. My love for him is missing; it was only my imagination.

Zainab Soogun

Fake Love

Missing, presumed dead, I held the remote control, which was smothered by a blanket of dust. I deeply pondered on whether I should turn the television on, which was peppered with bodies of flies, and see the chaos I left behind. I knew I couldn't give up as I had gone this far a little more wouldn't hurt, right? Anyway, I did. The television flickered and then I could see my mum's eyes flooding like a waterfall. I knew it meant nothing - I was nothing but a burden to them. Then why this fake love or was it true...?

Rytham Rasalawala (12)

Mini Saga

Why couldn't I remember? My mind was shaking. I didn't remember who took me. I didn't know why I was here. The last thing I remember was my eyes in darkness. Part of me was missing. Wasn't it? I was in prison. Abandoning myself like a lonely potato. I was a sloth, so slow. The place was empty... Suddenly, I heard a noise... The ransom note arrived. It had a picture of me. It said: 'Missing, presumed dead'. The money was gone, no reward or no number. I heard a noise. Wait, what was happening and why...?

Inayah Abbasi

An Omitted Perspective

Part of me is missing, an arm and a leg. She, is nowhere in sight. Isolated. Lying there in the mud and dirt, I scream and squirm. But to no avail. No-man's-land quivers from the presence of the heavy machinery, carrying and casting everything into the flames, incinerating all that it touches. Suddenly a white light shines on my decrepit self. My insides pulse as I am trapped in its metallic jaws. No escape. If only I could have at least one more day with her before this old bear is cast into the fires of this landfill...

Gene Simmonds (16)

Where Do Lost Things Go?

Where do lost things go? That book you left, that hat you dropped? Does it count as lost if you forget it? Lost in your mind, lost to your conscience. Or is that just careless? Selfish? Because all I know is my memories are no longer my own, my brain drained of any evidence of what defines me. As if they've been taken. I don't know who I am anymore. I can rummage through my thoughts as if they were paper. Blank paper.

All I hear is the same words everyone left hears, echoing around my skull.

Not. Your. Own.

Lilian Turner (16)

The Hidden

The cruel sun beat down, it's one malignant eye unblinking, the sky its sly collaborator without a wisp of cloud to soften the harsh rays. Me and my team ran wildly with a flock of 50 or so people, people who had gone missing for over five years without a trace, hidden away by the government who claimed that they were evil and brainwashed by a past virus that had wiped out half of the world's population. But we all know the government's unrevealed secret. What they had done to these people will cost them greatly.

Arzoo Nori (14)

Missing

Once, while three brave divers were going down in a submarine something tragic happened. They were diving and saw something on the seabed. It was too dark to see clearly and too far down, so they decided to go down in a submarine. As they were going, they were ready for anything. As they went deeper and deeper this strange object was still not clear. Before they came down in the submarine, they thought it was just a shipwreck but as they got closer its form changed. Eventually, they got to the bottom and never came back up.

Alex Delahaye (12)

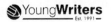

Position Vacant

I woke up and felt out of place. I looked around, everything was the same. I walked slowly, gliding my fingers along painted walls and clasping metal handles. Then I drummed along table and chairs and, I looked. Nothing. Every morning I look for you. You should be here, filling the silence. I see old photos and smile like an idiot. You're out of sight but you're never off my mind. I wondered if you think the same, if you miss me, or not. Maybe I should leave Post-Its reminding myself you're never coming back...

Noah Robinson (16)

Missing

They both sailed out to sea, all dressed in white. Yet only one returned, unknowing the whereabouts of the other. They searched and searched but to no avail. No phone, no letter, no word was spoken. No way of communicating. The only way she could think to find him was to retrace her steps, relive that day again, as much as she didn't want to. She put on her white outfit and ventured back out to sea. Hoping to catch one last precious glimpse of him. Nothing. As far as the eye could see. Looks like he's gone forever.

Alexia Wilson (13)

Was I A Mistake?

Running away from fear was a mistake. I'd much rather be seized, assaulted and sold. Black, sharp, earthly rooted hands grasped my ankles. Dragged to the core I plummetted. And now regurgitated from deathly worlds. I am a ghoul. Invisible. No longer touching things. Sucked through them and yet I seem pessimistic. They are not hindered. Parents who notice my absence but prioritise their integrity. Burning my absence with lies. She's safe with her aunty in Trinidad. I am missing, yet not found. Not even searched for.

Anya-Grace Nembhard (14)

A Homicidal Wanting

I feel breathless. Desperately, I search for it, I reach and claw and grapple, but it's gone. All my feeble pursuits do is aggravate an old wound, long time short of being fresh and formidably yielding. It's left me. Done its dirty work and left the residual traces of a certifiable life form to languish like flesh soaked in acid. I have never felt this way, as if I have been lacerated from my home. Not my veritable home. My reverie. The home in my mind. It came upon me one day, consumed me and now I crave for it...

Mia Rock (13)

The Shadow

It's been five years since I was announced missing, to most people it's just another cliche story; a typical teenager ran away from home after an argument with her parents and is missing the next day. Well, that's what they think happened, little do they know that I have been on the run for the past five years from him, his only goal is to kill me, no matter what. Why? What did I do wrong? I have learnt one thing: to stay hidden you have become a shadow. Never look for someone who doesn't want to be found.

Joanna Odumusi (14)

On The Tip Of My Tongue...

Tap, tap, tap. The sounds of the pen repeatedly hitting my desk was the only thing echoing through my head. I had been tasked to write a short story, no more than one hundred words. This was far less than a typical essay asked of me, so why was it so difficult? I normally had hundreds, no thousands, of different ideas coursing through my brain, yet now I drew a blank. I finally touched my pen to the page, only to instantly stop. A small dot of ink stared back at me, reminding me how difficult this task would be.

Tyler Dewick-Wilson

Missing

One normal Monday school morning, a class of students were very concerned about a new virus going around and nobody was sure of what was happening and thinking if it was going to be a problem. A boy called Marcus told everyone this virus won't be a big problem and not to fear, not knowing what would happen next.

The next morning, Marcus came to school with spots/rashes on his face, not knowing, it was this new virus so they locked the school and when it was re-opened everyone went missing and were never seen.

Lewis Nzekwe (12)

Kidnapped

I woke up to a scream. Isla was gone. I searched the whole house for her. She was nowhere to be found. I called her phone, but nobody answered, her phone was left in her room. I didn't know what to do. I called the police thinking the worst. Questions where running through my mind, had she been kidnapped? Did she leave on purpose? Was it my fault? I decided to search her room for any clues while I waited for the police to arrive. The police arrived and started looking with me. All we found was a suspicious note...

Hollie Mae Hughes (13)

New

Sweating. Scared. Alone. My bike screeched like the distant birds in the bleak trees. The water in the canal reverberated as it crashed against the banks. I had left behind the orphanage and myself. There was no turning back. I had finally reached the only tree along the track with a cloak of leaves. I rummaged around and soon my fingers clasped around the fake ID. Tonight was the moment that I had been waiting for. I was now missing. I had become an MIA. I could now start a new life. A new town. New people. A new me.

Erin Taylor (11)

I Have To Survive

I lay await, in the muddy leaves that carpeted the forest floor, for something, anything to happen. I had a bad feeling about this and look at where I am now: lost in the forest; split from any friends; running low on supplies; and fighting for my life. As I list these things, a wave of anxiety hits me like a boulder. "I'm gonna die out here," I whisper to myself. Just another victim, gone, missing in the jungle. I start running, adrenaline flowing through me. This cannot be my end, I have to survive...

Riya Swaminathan (12)

Friends

Once upon a time, lived a person named Jidou Higashifumi, he was not normal, he wanted to be lonely and not seen ever. However, when getting through school he had aced all of his tests, gaining the attention of his class and, eventually, one day saw some other children playing. He got the courage to ask them if he could be friends with them. Suddenly he realised he was missing something - friends! He spent the rest of his life happy, having a family and becoming the president of a large business in Akihabara, Japan.

Basar Kizildere (12)

Floating

I woke up as if it was an emergency, as if sleeping had become a dangerous thing. The atmosphere was encased with an empty silence that fuelled the darkness looming over me. As far as I could tell I was drowning alone in this sparkling pool of black; it felt like the universe was mine. I didn't know who I was or why I was there and any face my subconscious offered had as much resonance as a total stranger. The glitching from an old radio slowly crept up to my ears, the only word escaping it being 'help'!

Thalia Shola Remice (14)

Missing

Waking up, Day 14. It is still strange, everyone missing. I still remember the 25th December. When I wished everyone away. The streets are empty, I still do not feel safe. I broke down the doors to the shops. I hope they have food. My hunger is growing even more.

Day 27. I have finally finished all the food. There was even more than I expected, it does not matter now. I must leave the village, I cannot let it find me.

If it does, nobody will be left. I am scared. Steve Jones. Last man in the world...

Oliver Kent (13)

Vanished

Running through the beautiful lilac meadow filled with the scent of lavender. I couldn't think of a better place to be with my best friend on the last day of school. As I looked round just like the leaves on an autumn tree she had vanished. I frantically ran home not knowing I should have looked for her. I can still hear the shrill scream of her mother till this day. It haunts me along with the image of her standing at the end of my bed. Nobody knew what happened that day but she will always remain vanished...

Summer Mead

Running From The Mafia

They'll never find me, I hope... I've run away from my alcoholic dad in Russia, but I'm lost and very scared, I'm all alone but I've got to get away before papa finds me. I don't know where I'm going to run to, I've got no family, no friends, I'm not even meant to be outside. If the police find me, they will take me straight back to papa and fine him and he will be even more angry than normal, so I must be careful when I see police. I've found a place to sleep for tonight...

Oliver Lovelock (12)

Mission Gone Wrong

It had been a year. A year since they went missing. It was supposed to be a simple retrieval mission, but none of them came back. A team of five went into the town but only one managed to get out. Since then they haven't said a word, it's almost as if they couldn't that if they spoke of what happened something much worse would occur. The last thing I remember was saying goodbye to my baby sister, she volunteered for the mission, but now she was gone. My parents wouldn't say a thing. They blamed me.

Serena Whittlestone (15)

The Train

The train number was 628, I was on my way to visit my grandmother in London, I thought it would be at around 6:28, the train was supposed to arrive at King's Cross. When we arrived there was a huge crowd of people. Was this what it was usually like in London? I looked around for Grandma, strange how she wasn't there. I tried calling her but her phone didn't work, I got a taxi to her bungalow... She was strangely shocked to see me? Until I found out, it had been seven years since I got on that train...

Sophie Gillin (13)

The Lockdown

I walk into school and it looks like no one is here. I walk faster into the building and it still looks empty. I suddenly realise that no one is here. Confused, I check every classroom, the canteen, the library - all the places that should be full of people and noise. I go home and turn on the news. I cannot believe what I am seeing. My whole world has changed. A huge headline appears with the words: 'Schools closed across the UK'. I don't know how this is going to end but I feel safe with my family.

Sophie Edwards (12)

Powerless Exasperation

All the adrenaline had been drained from my body. The urge to run, the ability to fight. Drained. Gone! I fell to the ground, clenching my chest. The silence gripping me. Holding me down, no opportunity to rest. It was a whirlwind as I scrambled for escape but freedom wasn't in my reach. Only death was. I could sense him and his breath. I could feel him skulking. The terror holding me up. I froze and let the inside of me quake. Any slight control I had left of myself was crumbling at the speed of lightning.

Siân Phillips

I Will See Them Again

There was a time when all I could think about was the next step in life. Child to a teenager, teenager to adult. Now all I can think about is living. My parents had been deeply religious and never missed Sunday's service, but I believed and still believe there is no God. I think it's all in the mind. If God was real why do people die? It's just my outlook. People had always told me I am a very half-cup empty kind of person. Now there is nothing left but death. Will I see them again? Goodbye world.

Isabelle Embleton

The End Of The World

As I ran through the city I wondered to myself, *is this the end of the world?* Meteors crashed through buildings. The ground shook and people ran and screamed in terror. I ran into the house for cover. Suddenly, it started to shake. I looked out of the window and realised I was in a tornado. The wall ripped off the house and I was sucked outside. Debris, cars and signs flew past me. I grabbed onto a car as it was flung towards a lake. Before I was plunged into the ice-cold water everything went black.

Reece Walker (12)

Long Gone...

The house was empty! Anne was sleeping and snoring beside me. I could feel her cold feet under the sheepskin blanket. Lazily, I crept out of the sandy, heather beds. The sun was seeping through the cracks in the old, brick wall. Yesterday was six years since the car crash. Six years since Anne and I had been surviving alone. I could still hear the soft snoring of Anne as I opened the chest. It was gone! The last bit of money mum had left us was missing. How juvenile was I to think they would never find it!

Hiba Kola (13)

Missing

If I stop to dwell on my thoughts for even a second my face will drown with salty, cold, wet tears. They roll silently down my red cheeks into my sore cracked lips. My life was sweet and you left leaving a narrow, shallow hole which is gone forever. My heart is missing, so are you. I close my eyes and there you are calling my name but you're out of reach my love. Come back to me, your children are waiting for you patiently. If getting past this pain means forgetting you then I choose to suffer my love.

Mahdiya Noor Mahmood (13)

Gone

He was lost. Disappeared with only two traces - a large alien-like footprint and a long, windy trace of slime; a thick, oozing substance that was green.

After that we all ran - far away. None of us have ever bothered to return to the town we all once lived in. I was seven then... terrified and still am. Misery has hypnotised our people and so has fear. There is no hope. No happiness. Not many of us still live today, not after the next disappearance. We all ran and no one lives today but me and my family.

Amelie Coote (11)

Betrayal

Ow my head... as I begin to awaken, I feel an aching pain flow through my body. "Where am I?" A lost thought escapes my lips as I look around a familiar room, but where from? It is a basement of some sort, only one can presume. No windows, a flickering light and a bad feeling in the depths of my stomach "Yeah something seems off here..." Suddenly a door flings open, I cannot tell who it is until they speak and reality hits me. They have betrayed me, a person I thought I could trust...

Meghan Coleborn (15)

Hide-Or-Seek

One moment, a frenzy of tumultuous noise yet an empty, icy void of black and the next, silence, silence with a sprinkle of sweet bird song.

The little boy blinked and sat up in the warm, wet grass. He rolled his head to each side and yawned. It must be paradise: the blue skies, the lazy orange sun, the masses of lush vegetation. He was immediately drawn in and soon found himself lost. He hid. Then the sisters did the same. They too hid. However, the eldest climbed back through the open void. And sought.

Oliver Burrow (12)

Missing, Presumed Dead

Missing, Presumed Dead. That's what the signs with my face on say all around the town. That's what the newspaper with my picture on says. No one will find me. No one knows where I am. Apart from him. I won't write his name because if I do and I lose this note, I could lose everything. The one person I don't want to know my whereabouts knows exactly where I am. I haven't seen daylight in two weeks because I only sneak out at night. It's only safe to sneak out at night...

Sophia Nelson (13)

Missing

When I look in the mirror at night I still see the shadows of the unnameable pain and torture. I was not missing, I was stolen and hidden away from my parents, along with many other helpless children cruelly tricked. In my nightmarish dreams at night I am there. I remember it. I see it. I hear it. I feel it. How my best friend was never seen alive again after that dreaded night. And how if I had not managed to escape I would have joined her terrible fate and taken to where all the good lost things go.

Mya Kent (12)

The Borrower

"I placed the button on the side and now it's gone!"
In the depths of your house, just behind the skirting board,
lives a tiny little man called a borrower dressed in red. You
never see him, he is invisible to the human eye, here is proof.
If you have a pet at home then you know that they
can be crazy sometimes, you think that they are trying to
play with you but they are actually trying to catch the
borrower with a lost item in hand, a token or a coin, a piece
of ribbon or... a button!

Amelia Drummond-Harris (11)

The Money

The money was gone. I knew it as soon as I walked into the room. The chairs were turned, papers were flung around and glass littered the floor. My breathing quickened as I tried to think of another plan, but the deadline was in a couple hours and I was five thousand pounds short. Where was I going to get that much money? I threw some clothes into a bag and propped it onto my shoulder. I had to run. I headed to the train station, hopped on the first train and then looked around. Then I spotted him...

Joana Cabaca

Delusion

Life was a prison. Nothing gave me hope. I longed for a better life away from the tormenting, judgemental atmosphere. I bought a one-way ticket out, turns out that ticket brought me deeper in. I was deluded with this town in my mind, trapped. I had to do something. I had to crush every morsel of life left in that town. So, I took a one-way ticket back. Back to the beginning. I arrived in the town a maniac, a freak. I saw a girl. I drew nearer. Closer. I put a blade to her head, this was the start...

Finn Shuttleworth (10)

The Missing Spy

The spy has disappeared, we don't know where he is, we can't track him down. What are we going to do? The secret USB stick is missing as well. It was holding all the answers for this mission, maybe our spy got caught but we don't know, the mission has failed. All we need to do is find the missing spy because we need him. We need to make sure he has not joined the other side; he might even be spying on us. What are we going to do?

Mission brief: Can you help us find the missing spy?

Morgan Mates (11)

Hiding

The money is mine. I stole it because he hated me. I have escaped to Amsterdam. The police will never find me. I am hiding in an abandoned casino, it's safe but I have move soon.

30th April: It's time. I would have to ask for direct routes since I am a refuge to the Netherlands. As I walk to the shop a Dutch shepherd starts to pound towards me. I can't outrun dogs. Soon the dog catches up. He crunches on my leg. I fall over in agony and before I know it... I am the dog's meal.

Abdullah Ahmad (12)

Missing

Dark. I didn't know where I was. The place had this weird rotten smell. I was held hostage on a moist, rigid surface. All I wanted to know was who the man in the shadows keeping me captive was. I asked him what he wanted from me, but he started to laugh. All he said was that he wanted to hunt everyone 'special' as am I. Then I knew: he was a hunter and he knew I was one of those terrible creatures. A murderer. A vampire. He wanted to kill me... Then my witchy friend came to rescue me.

Mateea Sivriu (19)

Who Am I?

Why can't I remember? Who am I? Where am I? I have so many questions running through my head. I was in a strange room: it was pale pink with a big white wardrobe to the side. The name Maya was plastered in big letters across the wall. "Is that my name?" I wondered. Then what looked like a diary fell onto the ground. I opened it with curiosity. I saw the word help! Then it all came back to me like a gushing river. I had been kidnapped! I was missing! I had to get out; I needed help.

Amelia Lewis (12)

Missing

I decided to run away from home. Go far away from all the treacherous people and their wicked schemes. I'd wanted to do this for a long time but just didn't have the guts. I decided the only way to get away from them was if I fled the country, so I stole my uncle's credit card when he was fast asleep and used it to buy a one-way ticket to a small city in Ohio. Twenty-four hours later, I had arrived in my new home. They would never get to me now. They would assume that I was missing.

Aarna Patel (12)

Disappearance Of Kelly

My heart pounds in my stomach as the van swerves from side to side, my arm crashing against the window at every corner they turn. I can't see a thing, they blindfolded me, and all I can smell is the cloud of cigar smoke circling round my head and a man's BO. Why did I trust them? Something hard hit me right round the back of the head and I blacked out.
I wake up sitting in a chair, inside a dimmed room with four men. "Right, shall we get to work?" One steps towards me...

Caitlyn Gallagher-Blake (11)

The Socks

Disbelief coursed through my body as I watched the school bus drive away. I stood there horrified. By the time I had come to my senses, the school bus was gone. My socks, where were they? Last night before bed I made sure I put out my clothes for the next day, however, I awoke to everything but my socks. Outside I heard a crash so I peered down to see a cat jump onto our bin, knocking it over and spilling the contents. On top of the pile of trash I couldn't believe what I saw - my socks.

Jimisola Okuwobi (12)

The Missing Grave

On a Sunday stroll we passed the graveyard. As we passed it, Charlie, our Labrador, dashed off in a fit and bolted straight into the graveyard. As I walked to Charlie, I stopped by a grave. I looked. It had my name on it. It said I'd died at the age of five. It was open. I sprinted all the way back home. I dashed through the door that was open and I stopped. A decrepit man was standing there. He said, "This is my house! I am you. I lived in a grave!" Then he drew out a sword...

Leon Gamper (11)

SOS Message

Hello, is this thing on? My name is Monty and about two weeks ago I was flying over the Pacific Ocean when the plane's engine failed and the last thing I can remember was getting into a life raft and floating away. Then I was waking up on this island and trying to make a shelter for myself. Food is low and the only water here is salty and the chances of me surviving a week longer is about five per cent. If anyone finds this it will probably be too late but tell my family I loved them.

Monty Hulbert (12)

Maison Des Esclaves

Missing, presumed dead, at the moment, I wish I was. They were coming and nobody could stop them. It all started a year ago, back on Goree Island, in 1826, where I was held at The Maison des Esclaves (The House of Slaves). I was put on a ship, bound for a new world where I was bought by a lady named Sasha Vahn. She was cruddy and rude, she would lock me up for days if one of the cows from the local farm didn't give her as much milk as usual! I had to do something, but what? Run!

Rubi Merrell (13)

The Mystery Of The Missing...

Tim was going to his football club but he felt unsafe on the way. It was very quiet and wasn't like an ordinary day. The streets were empty, only a van passed by. As his friend John was crossing the road to him, a black van drove by and suddenly he had vanished. Tim was confused and worried about him. As he tried to follow the van, it cut the corner and was gone. What was happening? Was this real? What was he going to do? He hid behind the bush and felt someone grab him...

Khrish Deugi (12)

Escape

Could it be? Surely not, I must be sure. The door is open, this is my chance, my first and probably last chance in ten long years! I am petrified at the thought of leaving because I know what will happen if he catches me, but I must try. I slowly ease the door open. Sunlight falls down on me for the first time in years, I am blinded by it but there is no time to let my eyes adjust. I shakily run towards the gate. I really think I could make it. But then, he roars my name...

Naideen Elle Dailly (12)

1000 Tears

1000 tears is the sound in my ears. Crying, wailing, mind ailing. Blackout.

Where am I? I thought when I awoke, for not a bone but a mind had broke. I knew what was missing, but then, I realised I might not see it again. I realised the place I saw was all in my head. I fell asleep and woke up in bed. But only that place was all in my head. My friend had died in the war I fled. I hope to see my friend again, but like lost and found I'll have to wait until then.

Brandon Ellis

Missing

I have gone missing for a few days. I can't get back home, but I need to, my parents are worried. I feel my voice is missing, my life is missing. What do I do? My whole life has gone, I have no chance anymore. I should really head home, but shall I? Yes, I will. I start walking back in the dark. It is also raining. I will walk for two hours and not return till midnight.

Two hours later I return home. I open the front door and sneak upstairs into my nice comfy bed.

Dane Brett (12)

Gone

I walked into Sylvia's room to wake her up one morning as usual, but she wasn't there. Her bed was all tidy though she never made her bed. The window was open - she wouldn't have a window open even if she was boiling. It was all very strange. Sylvia wasn't the type of girl who liked to be alone and would always tell me if she was going out. I stepped out into the street. The air was freezing cold. The hairs on my neck stood on end. Where was my daughter?

Jessica Williamson (13)

Missing

I was running into the green lush forest. I was chasing a bright light. I was drawn to it was like a magnet to a fridge. However, I could not catch it, it was going to fast. As I gradually got deeper and deeper into the forest I tripped on a rock in the floor. I looked up and realised the sky was as dark as space. I pulled my phone out to text my mum but then I sliced my finger on the shattered glass. I used the light from the front of the screen. I was still lost...

Cohyn Williams (12)

Missing...

One dull night I walked out of my house because my sensors went off. I went to turn it off but when I went outside I wasn't outside my house, I was in an abandoned forest so I decided to try to find a river to survive and get some fish. I found a river. I heard a loud roar behind me. I turned to look at what it was but I saw nothing. Then I quickly hid in some bushes as soon as I could. It was an animal. It looked at me...

Suddenly, I appeared in my bed.

Eryk Grzegorz Wojewodzki (13)

Where Are The Socks?

What in the world just happened? Yesterday, my feet were feeling a bit cold, so I decided to find some pair of socks in the drawer in my room. However, I noticed that there were no socks whatsoever. Initially, I assumed that my socks were still in the washing basket or the drying room, but then I checked in both areas and they were not there. I tried asking my mum and dad, but they were both wondering the same thing... *Where are the socks?*

Fikile Soko (11)

Shadows

She was everywhere, yet nowhere and all I could do was wait. Missing a lifetime ago and vanished completely. Hopes and fears colliding like atoms in space. Shadows creeping in corners, shivering down my spine. Leaving no trace of life, empty and unknown. I felt her presence like she was next to me, a hollow feeling inside my heart. Her ghostly voice drifting on a soft breeze, but she was never there, until one day I got a call...

Evie May Phipps (13)

Missing

Lost. All alone. And no one to help. No one who cares. Is this what I get? All I wanted was freedom and a good home. My paws pitter-patter like the pattering of raindrops on a leaf. My stomach growls angrily as I soldier on in the cold and the dark. Isolated from all of humanity, all I can hope for is the kindness of a lone stranger...

Hawwaa' Bint Mahmood (16)

YOUNG WRITERS INFORMATION

We hope you have enjoyed reading this book – and that you will continue to in the coming years.

If you're a young writer who enjoys reading and creative writing, or the parent of an enthusiastic poet or story writer, do visit our website **www.youngwriters.co.uk**. Here you will find free competitions, workshops and games, as well as recommended reads, a poetry glossary and our blog. There's lots to keep budding writers motivated to write!

If you would like to order further copies of this book, or any of our other titles, then please give us a call or order via your online account.

Young Writers
Remus House
Coltsfoot Drive
Peterborough
PE2 9BF
(01733) 890066
info@youngwriters.co.uk